# Allie, the Christmas Spider

BY

Shirley Menendez

ILLUSTRATED BY

Maggie Kneen

# Allie, the Christmas Spider

DUTTON CHILDREN'S BOOKS

New York

*Library of Congress Cataloging-in-Publication Data*
Menendez, Shirley.
Allie, the Christmas spider / by Shirley Menendez ; illustrated by Maggie Kneen—1st ed.
p. cm.
Summary: A family's sparce Christmas is brightened, thanks to the efforts of a special spider.
ISBN 0-525-46860-9
[I. Spiders—Fiction. 2. Christmas—Fiction.] I. Kneen, Maggie, ill. II. Title.
PZ7.M5265 Al 2002   [E]—dc21  2001040398

Published in the United States 2002 by Dutton Children's Books,
a division of Penguin Putnam Books for Young Readers
345 Hudson Street, New York, New York 10014
www.penguinputnam.com

Designed by Alyssa Morris
Printed in China
First Edition

1   3   5   7   9   10   8   6   4   2

For Albert
S.M.

For Angela, Ceilidh, and Robert
M.K.

It was Christmas Eve. Soft flakes of snow fell on the little town. Colored lights twinkled in the shop windows.

Shoppers dashed from store to store, buying last-minute presents. Beth held her mother's hand as they hurried home. She gazed longingly at the stores they passed.

When they reached the toy shop, Beth had to stop in front of the window. "Look, Mama," she said. "I wish I could have a doll like that for Christmas."

Mama put her arm around Beth. "And I wish we could buy one for you. But we have very little money to spend this year, and there are so many other things we need. I know it's hard. . . ."

"No, it's all right," Beth said, giving her mother a reassuring smile. "I understand."

"That's a good girl," said Mama. "We'll have a great Christmas, you'll see. Now let's get home—we have a lot of preparing to do!"

As Beth and Mama came up the front steps, Allie watched them through the living-room window. Allie was a spider who had been living with Beth's family for the last few months, catching bugs that dared to stray into the house.

Mama put down her packages and said, "Beth, I need to get dinner ready. Would you do a little cleaning before Papa gets home? He's bringing a special surprise, remember?"

Allie wondered what the surprise would be. She skittered into the other room to watch Mama prepare supper, as she did every evening. This was Allie's favorite time of the day.

Beth took out the broom and began sweeping crumbs off the floor. Allie closed her eyes and enjoyed the smell of dinner cooking. She didn't see the broom coming straight for her. Beth accidentally swept Allie into the dustpan.

Thankfully, when Beth took the dustpan outside to dump out the crumbs, she spotted the tiny spider. Beth gently put the dustpan down and allowed Allie to crawl over the side. Allie dashed back inside.

Allie reached her corner safely and settled into her web, still trembling from her close call. Just when she was beginning to feel better, she saw Beth coming toward her again, this time with a dustcloth. Beth had let Allie go before, but would this be the end of her?

Beth wiped the table and stopped when she saw Allie's web glistening in the window. She peered at it closely, fascinated by the pattern Allie had made.

Allie was so scared she didn't know whether to run or sit still. Then Beth blew on the web, and it began to sway. Allie had to hold on tight to keep from falling out. Beth covered her mouth and whispered, "I'm sorry. I didn't mean to frighten you. Please go back to sleep. You'll be my little secret."

Just then the front door opened, and Beth's father called, "Come and see what I found in the woods!" Beth squealed with excitement. Allie hurried into the living room to see what all the fuss was about. Papa carried in a large pine tree and placed it in a corner by the window. It was so tall it almost reached the ceiling.

"Let's decorate it!" Beth cried, skipping around the tree.

"Not yet, young lady," said her mother. "After we eat."

Beth wasn't the only impatient one. Allie could hardly wait until supper was over. She decided to climb up onto the mantel, where she could get a better view. She hid behind a candle and stayed very still so no one would notice her.

Beth was the first to return to the living room. She carried a
big bowl of popcorn. Mama brought a needle and thread. As
Beth handed her pieces of popcorn, her mother pushed the needle

through and slid them onto the thread. When the string of popcorn was long enough to stretch across the living room, Papa wrapped the chain around and around the tree.

Then Papa brought out what he called "the ornament box." The family began digging through it, stopping now and then to hold up a colorful object and say, "Remember this one?"

After hanging a few of her favorite ornaments on the tree, Beth climbed onto her mother's lap. "Will there be presents under the tree tomorrow morning?"

Mama smiled. "You'll just have to wait and see. Now you'd better get to bed. Papa will tuck you in."

"Can't I stay up until Christmas comes?" Beth begged.

Papa shook his head. "Come upstairs and I'll read you a bed-time story." He lifted Beth onto his shoulders and climbed the steps two at a time.

Allie watched Mama go to the closet and bring out some presents. One was a rag doll Mama had made for Beth. Allie knew that Mama had worked long and hard on it. They had spent many a night together—Mama in her chair, sewing scraps of cloth, and Allie in the corner, spinning a web.

Papa soon returned to the living room and helped Mama arrange the few gifts under the tree. "I hope Beth won't be too disappointed tomorrow," he said. "I wish we could have bought her some toys."

Mama tried to sound cheerful. "There will be other years when things will be better."

They stood silently in front of the Christmas tree for a while. Even with the popcorn string and ornaments, it still seemed bare. Papa sighed. "Maybe everything will look brighter in the morning." He turned out the lights, and they went upstairs to bed.

Allie scuttled out of her hiding place but didn't know where to go next. She was sorry to hear the sadness in Mama's and Papa's voices, and she hated to think that her new friend Beth might be disappointed. She wished she had presents to offer the family. But what could a spider give?

She looked over at the Christmas tree. She had never seen a tree inside before, but she had to admit that it made the room feel cozier. In fact, in the glow of the dying firelight, the popcorn strings even looked a bit like a spiderweb. . . .

At that moment, Allie realized what she could give Beth's family for Christmas. She grew so excited that she began to dance, and she almost fell off the mantel.

Collecting herself just in time, Allie dropped down from a line of spider silk and swung over to the tree. She landed on one of its branches and began to spin more silk. She attached spokes from one branch to another and spun silver round and round to make a pattern.

Allie went from branch to branch, swinging and spinning. Her eight legs worked quickly and steadily. Finally she reached the very top of the tree. As tired as she was, she knew that the web at the top had to be her best. She pushed on, swinging and spinning.

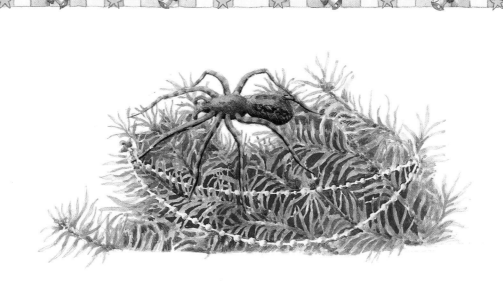

At last she was done. And her last web was indeed her finest.

From the top of the tree, Allie could see the sunrise outside. She had been working so hard she lost track of time. Beth and her parents would be up soon. Allie had barely enough energy left to jump to her line and crawl back up to the mantel. She took her place behind the candle again.

On Christmas morning, Beth was the first one out of bed. She
hurried downstairs to see if there were presents under the tree.
But when she reached the living room, she stopped short. Delicate

silver patterns covered the tree from top to bottom. They sparkled in the early-morning sunlight.

"Mama, Papa, come see!" Beth called. "Our tree—it's magical!"

Beth's parents also stared in amazement. "Who could have . . . ?" they asked.

Beth giggled. "I think I know who did it. We met yesterday. I almost swept her up by mistake, then I let her go."

"Looks like she wanted to say thank you," said Papa.

"And now we have her to thank," said Mama.

"It's the most beautiful Christmas ever," said Beth, "thanks to the Christmas Spider."

Allie was so tired she had trouble staying awake long enough to see the family's reaction. Their words made her very happy. Never had her efforts been so admired. Never had she felt so much at home.

As she drifted off in her mantel hiding place, Allie, the Christmas Spider, thought: This is a good spot for a new web. And it has a great view of the tree.

She slept long and hard, dreaming about her next work of art.